A Gift For:

_____

From:

_____

Published by Hallmark Gift Books,
a division of Hallmark Cards, Inc.,
Kansas City, MO 64141
Visit us on the Web at Hallmark.com.

Editorial Director: Delia Berrigan
Editor: Kara Goodier
Art Director: Chris Opheim
Designer: Scott Swanson
Production Designer: Dan Horton

ISBN: 978-1-63059-644-6
KCX1012

Made in China
0719

This Is Snow Time for Sleeping!

Z Z Z Z Z

Hallmark

A STORY FROM THE HALLMARK HOLIDAY SERIES
Written by Andrew Blackburn Illustrated by Mike Esberg

Inside a small house perched atop a big hill,
lived a snowboy with spunk, and his name was Chill Bill.
As visions of snowy dreams danced through his head,
not ONE of those dreams involved going to bed.

Welcome
to
Driftdale

"It's bedtime!" said Dad. "Chill Bill, hurry along.
Put your snowjamas on! Sing your tooth-brushing song!
A snowkid needs sleep to grow up big and strong."

"But Dad!" Chill Bill said, "Now is no time for sleep.
I made Santa promises that I must keep!
I'm helping check in on his friends this December.
He's busy this month, as I'm sure you remember."

"And who," asked his mom, "might these Santa-friends be?"
"The Cane-Deer are first!" Chill Bill said. "Come and see!"
They're used to their once-daily candy cane rations.
We can't let them starve! Do you have no compassion?"

So off they all set—Chill Bill looked left and right.

But sadly, the Cane-Deer were nowhere in sight.

"What gives?" Chill Bill said. "I just saw them last night!"

"Don't worry," said Dad. "Hey, pretending is fun! But let's go to bed, since your work here is done."

"Done?" Chill Bill said. "No, I'm just getting started!"
It seemed that his job wasn't for the fainthearted.
"I've got to go check on the Great Cocoa Dragon.
We're doing repairs on her hot chocolate wagon!"

They arrived at the den, with Chill Bill as their guide,
but there wasn't a Great Cocoa Dragon inside.
"And I'm guessing," said Dad, "she'd be tricky to hide."

"But I've met her," said Chill Bill. "It's not in my head!"
But his parents insisted they go back for bed.

"Not yet!" said Chill Bill. "Though I know you're exhausted.
I have to get Gingy the Narwhal re-frosted!
I help him do touch-ups on Mondays and Fridays
to keep all his gumdrops from drooping off sideways.

Just wait 'til you see him—you don't want to miss it!"
So his parents agreed to just one more quick visit.

Chill Bill searched all around. In the snow. In the water.

He asked an ice dolphin and three arctic otters.

He called a professional gingerbread spotter.

But no frosted Narwhal bobbed up from the lake.

"This," said Chill Bill, "is some kind of mistake."

"You know," said his mom, "I bet they're all exploring!"
Santa won't mind—staying put would be boring."
And though scenes of snow-creatures danced in his head,
Chill Bill said with a yawn, "OK, let's go to bed."

And soon, they were back in their house on the hill—
one Mom and one Dad and one sleepy Chill Bill.
"I'm sorry we missed all your friends," his mom said
as they gathered to read one last book before bed.

"That's okay," Chill Bill said. "Besides, nothing is better
than staying up late making stories together!"

If this chilly adventure warmed your heart,
or if perhaps you just liked the art,
we would love to hear from you.

Please write a review at Hallmark.com,
e-mail us at booknotes@hallmark.com,
or send your comments to:

Hallmark Book Feedback
P.O. Box 419034
Mail Drop 100
Kansas City, MO 64141